SHEILA O'FLANAGAN

THREE'S A CROWD

WITHDRAWN
FROM
STOCK

Sheila O'Flanagan is the author of over a dozen internationally bestselling novels. In her spare time she plays competitive badminton.

NEW ISLAND *Open Door*

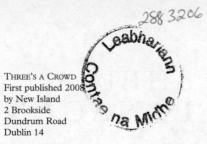

2883206

THREE'S A CROWD
First published 2008
by New Island
2 Brookside
Dundrum Road
Dublin 14

A version of this Open Door Series book was first published in 2006 by Hodder Headline Ireland as part of the short story collection, *Connections*.

www.newisland.ie

A CIP catalogue record for this book is available from the British Library.

ISBN 978-1-905494-85-9

New Island receives financial assistance from
The Arts Council (An Chomhairle Ealaíon), Dublin, Ireland.

Printed in Ireland by ColourBooks
Cover design by Artmark

1 3 5 4 2

Dear Reader,

On behalf of myself and the other contributing authors, I would like to welcome you to the sixth Open Door series. We hope that you enjoy the books and that reading becomes a lasting pleasure in your life.

Warmest wishes,

Patricia Scanlan.

Patricia Scanlan
Series Editor

We nearly missed the flight from London.

Our connection from Dublin had been delayed and we were late. I told Harry it might happen but he didn't believe me. He told me that I was getting into a state over nothing.

'Everything will be fine,' he said calmly. 'We've still got plenty of time.'

Of course, I wanted to believe him. But when we finally arrived at Gatwick Airport, there was a problem with the check-in computer system. There were long queues everywhere.

The longest queue was for our airline. And we were at the back of it. It was moving very, very slowly indeed. I didn't think we would reach the desk before our flight was called.

'Don't be so silly,' Harry told me. Even though he told me not to be silly, he sounded a bit worried himself. 'There's buckets of time.'

Well, of course there wasn't buckets of time. We shuffled along in the queue. I tried to be calm but I was really panicked. Harry tried not to looked panicked himself. But he kept glancing at his watch whenever he thought I wasn't looking. The minutes ticked by. Both of us were worried. Missing the flight would be a disaster!

It wasn't a good start, I thought. I was really mad at him, even though it wasn't totally his fault. But I wished he had done what I wanted and travelled from Dublin to London the night before. We could have had a lovely night in one of the airport hotels. We could have got to check-in in plenty of time. We could have been at the front of this queue, not the back.

I sighed deeply as we moved forward again. The dress I was carrying over my arm weighed a ton. It was coming with me as cabin baggage. I had had a row with them in Dublin about it. I told them that it was my fairy-tale wedding dress. It had cost almost as much as the trip itself. There was no way I was letting it out of my sight. In the end they said OK. But I was still tense from arguing with them.

Everything would be fine once we got on the plane. We were going to our perfect wedding place. Well, actually, everything would be fine *if* we got on the plane! I tried not to think about missing the flight. I had been looking forward to this week for the past twelve months. It had to be perfect.

The brochure was called *Weddings in Paradise*. The minute I read it I knew that it was exactly right for me and Harry. I wanted to get married on the beach in the sun. Some people said that the trendy thing to do now was go to Eastern Europe. Maybe get married in the winter. In the snow. But I wanted to get married in paradise.

I imagined walking barefoot along the white sands in my white dress. I imagined my blonde hair falling in curls around my face. I imagined myself looking beautiful. OK, I knew that I probably wouldn't look beautiful. I'm not really that pretty! But it was a nice image all the same.

The plan had been for just the two of us to go. We wanted to avoid a big wedding in Dublin. We wanted to avoid the frenzy. Anyway, Harry had been married before. I had seen his wedding photos. I thought it looked like the wedding from hell. There was a big crowd of friends and family. They all seemed to be pushing and shoving each other. The bride looked nervous. She was beside Harry's mother in one photo. Maybe that's why she looked nervous! Harry's mother looked a bit scary. She had an orange tan, for starters. She was wearing a fancy purple suit and a matching purple hat. The hat had a huge peacock feather sticking out of it. As I looked at those photographs, I could see why the marriage had gone up in smoke. No bride likes coming second to her mother-in-law's hat.

Harry's first marriage had lasted three years. I was hoping that ours would last forever. I was sure it would. I loved Harry. He was The One. He was kind and considerate and funny. He treated me like an expensive jewel. Honestly. Most of the time, anyway. All my friends loved Harry too. He was impossible not to love. Well, unless you were Karen – wife number one. She had once left a nasty message on his mobile phone. She had called him a self-centred, self-obsessed, selfish rat. I resented Karen. Harry paid a lot of money to her. Mostly for their child. I didn't resent money for their little girl. But sometimes Karen asked for extra. I hated how much he seemed to give her.

But Harry never let it get him down. The thing is, Harry always looks on the bright side. He is the life and soul of any party. He has a good word to say about everyone. He likes being surrounded by friends. He cares about family too. He doesn't see much of his brother and sister. But that's not his fault. They live outside Dublin. It's hard for them to visit all the time.

Harry is also devoted to his mother. His father had died a few years before

I came on the scene and he takes care of her. He drops in on his way home from work and runs errands for her. I'm making him sound a bit too perfect, maybe. He wasn't perfect. Of course he wasn't. But he was perfect for me.

He loved going out. But he knew that I couldn't always go too. I'm a nurse. I work shifts. That means I can't always go on the lash. If I have to be in work, I don't want to have a hangover. I don't want to poison a patient by mistake. My last boyfriend, Carl, called me a party pooper. I wasn't. I'm not.

After all, I allowed my tiny private wedding to turn into a massive party. That's not the action of a party pooper. To be honest, I wasn't exactly mad about how it happened. It wasn't really what I wanted. The reason for going to the Caribbean in the first place was to have a small wedding. A romantic wedding for the two of us. But then Harry said it would be a pity to be all alone. It would be nice to share our day with friends.

'We don't need anyone else,' I told him.

'No, absolutely. But it would be nice, don't you think? It would be nice to celebrate with some people we know? Just a few of them.'

He had a point. It did seem a bit sad to go all that way and then sit down for a meal on our own. Maybe it would be better to share it with friends. But I wasn't sure how many friends would want to come. After all, travelling to the Caribbean just before Christmas would be expensive. I guessed only Harry's friends might be able to come. Mine wouldn't have been able to afford it. Harry's mates seemed to be better off than mine. They were all in jobs that paid well. They had cars and apartments. They seemed to take lots of holidays. None of my friends earned a lot of money, although we all wished we did!

We decided not to ask our families. Mine is huge and you know how it is. If you leave someone out, you've insulted them for life. Even if they didn't really want to come in the first place. Even if they hated the idea of travelling so far for a wedding. So it was easier to ask nobody at all. I talked it over with Mum. She was perfectly happy. She had done four weddings already with my sisters and brothers. She was easygoing about missing this one. Besides, my younger sister loves big weddings. When she gets married she'll ask everyone!

Harry thought his mother might like to come. But I told him it wouldn't be much fun for Gloria. She would probably feel odd. The only parent

among all of our friends. I didn't want her to feel left out. Although I wasn't sure that she *would* feel that way. Gloria gets on with people, just like Harry. She goes out a lot. But this was different. Everyone would be much younger than her.

Anyway, she knew that this was a low-key second wedding. Harry said she understood. But I think she would have liked to wear her hat again! Gloria likes hats. She has lots of them. She once won Best Dressed Lady at the Horse Show. All of her friends were very impressed. She said it meant her taste was excellent and that she was very stylish. I wasn't so sure. I know I sound bitchy here, but … when you see Gloria you think 'mutton dressed as lamb'. I know you can't judge someone on how they look. But sometimes it's hard not to.

In the end, twelve of Harry's friends said that they would come to the wedding. I was very surprised. I thought that only three or four would come. Then the beautiful White Sands hotel told us that they would give us a special rate on the rooms. But we needed two more people to come to get it. So I asked my own friends, Sarah and Dee, if they could come at the special rate. I didn't want all the guests at our wedding to be Harry's friends. I liked them. I really did. But I wanted friends of my own. I was beginning to feel outnumbered by Harry's friends. It was like it was Harry's wedding, not mine. Well, I thought, it was actually *our* wedding!

We didn't all travel together. Some of Harry's friends were to be on the same flight as us. But the others were taking a different flight. Sarah and Dee were on the other one. It was with a different airline and it left later in the day. (We should have picked that one ourselves. Then we would have had plenty of time!)

But Rob, Ken, Dave, Winston, Katy and Bella were with us in the big long queue.

'Don't worry,' said Katy as she saw me check my watch again and again. 'They won't go without us.'

They nearly did. It was getting very late. I was totally panicked. I could hardly stand still I was so worried. Then people from the airline began calling out for everyone on our flight. There were a lot of us. They got us to the top of the queue. Next thing we were at the check-in desk. Harry was smiling at me and telling me that he had said all along that there was no need to worry. I only stopped worrying when we got the boarding cards.

I like the fact that Harry is an optimistic person. It's very nice. I'm always looking for the snags in life. I can't help myself. I want to be as laid back and cheerful about things as him. But it's just not in my nature. I reckon that this was what drew us together. My half-empty glass and his half-full one. Oh, look, I'm not that bad really. But I'm the sort of person things go wrong for. Like I usually bring my umbrella to work every day because I think it's going to rain. It never does. But on the day I forget my umbrella – then it rains. In my head I'm always prepared for the worst. But I like to hope that the best will happen.

The worst happened at the boarding gate. The stewardess took one look at my gorgeous dress and told me that it would have to go in the hold. I told her that it would end up there over my dead body. She said it wouldn't fit in the overhead bin. And, she added, even if it did, it would get crushed by the hand baggage of the other passengers. We stared at each other for two full minutes before I agreed to let her hold on to the dress. She promised to bring it up to the plane when everyone had boarded. Then she would ask the steward to find a place for it in the cabin.

The row with the stewardess had upset me. I was still angry when we took our seats. They were at the very back of the plane, in row sixty-four. Then a steward came down to us. He told us that there was space for us in the premium cabin, where my dress was waiting for me.

'You see,' said Harry as we sat down in the wider seats with more leg room and took up their offer of free champagne. 'There was no need to worry about anything.'

It was a great flight, though I wished we had been on our own in the premium cabin. Rob and Bella and the others kept coming up to us and slagging us about our upgrade and our wedding. I couldn't help thinking that some of the other people in the premium section were getting fed up with all the visitors.

'It's just that they're a bit … well … over the top,' I explained to Harry.

'They're happy. They're fun. They're looking forward to a great week.'

'Me too,' I said. Then I freaked out because I discovered that Katy had spilled champagne onto the ends of my wedding dress. (It had a seat to itself. Although it was covered in plastic, the ends peeked out.) I spotted it just as we were coming in to land. That meant I didn't really get to see the green island sticking out of the blue sea. I was too busy having a quiet fit. But by the time we landed, I had been comforted enough by Harry to feel that maybe things weren't so bad. But I kept the dress close to me after that. I didn't want anything else to happen to it. I was more than relieved when we were finally alone in our gorgeous hotel room.

'This is the life.' Harry stretched out on the huge bed with its white canopy. 'Couldn't you just live here forever?'

I nodded.

'Though I suppose you'd get fed up with it after a while,' he said.

'Rubbish.' I smiled at him as I lay down beside him. 'How could anyone get tired of paradise?'

'Indeed,' he remarked as he kissed me. 'Total paradise.'

★

Paradise was fantastic. Really it was. Blue skies, blue seas and the gorgeous white sands. Even though I felt a bit odd being in such a big gang, it was fun. I would have preferred more time alone with Harry. But we had our whole lives to be alone together. He said this the second night when we were dancing together. This was celebration time. We should live it up to the max.

It was nice to have Dee and Sarah with me when I went to the spa to book some beauty treatments ahead of the big day. A local girl named Marilou was going to do me up. She was absolutely lovely. She promised to make me her best bride ever. I guessed she said that to all of her brides. But I wanted to believe her. The hotel was very popular for weddings. So far there had been a wedding every single day! As I left the spa, I smiled at another girl who was getting married at White Sands too. Then I went back to the beach to top up my tan. I was going to be a gorgeous bride (hopefully). This would be the best wedding ever. I was the luckiest girl in the world.

*

The bombshell dropped the following evening. We were all in the Green

Garden restaurant. Our tables were grouped together and surrounded by tropical plants. Winston was giving us the inside track on the celebrity trial of the year. Winston was one of Harry's nicest friends. He was a barrister and had lots of great stories. This one was about a top Irish pop star who had been sued by her driving instructor. He had claimed sexual harassment. The pop star had won the case. Winston said that the whole truth had not come out in court. Winston told the story in a very funny way. I couldn't really imagine him as a barrister. I couldn't imagine him being hard on witnesses. But Harry said that he was really good at it and that he could be very tough. We were all laughing at the story when suddenly Harry stood up and cried, 'Mum!' His voice carried right across the restaurant.

Well, I didn't think he was actually calling his mother. Gloria was supposed to be tucked up in her gorgeous County Dublin home. So I wondered what on earth he was going on about. And then I followed his eyes and my jaw dropped. Because there she was, standing at the entrance to the Green Garden. She was wearing a blue silk dress which clung to her curvy body. Gloria is sixty-two but she doesn't look a day over twenty-two. Sorry, that's a complete lie because she does. But she hides her age well. She has had 'work' done to her eyes and her forehead. And she has had collagen injections in her lips. (She has a bit of a trout pout. I wouldn't have liked to be her husband with those lips coming at me. So maybe just as well he had popped his clogs.) However, from a distance, Gloria looked young. Up close, of course, her wrinkly hands gave her away. So did her gleaming false teeth.

'What the …' I stared as she walked across the room.

'Oh, Mum!' Harry gave her a bear hug and lifted her off her feet. 'I'm so happy to see you.' He turned to me. 'Well, Jen,' he said, 'what do you think?'

I was still staring. 'What are you doing here?' I asked.

Gloria laughed. 'How could I stay away?' she asked brightly. 'I wanted to be here when my baby married the love of his life.'

There was an amused chuckle around the table. She beamed at everyone. 'I know you all think I'm far too young to be his mother,' she said. (I swear to God she believed her own words.) 'But I couldn't stay away.'

I frowned. 'But … but … you never said anything!' Then I looked accusingly at Harry. 'You never said anything either.'

'Of course not,' he said. 'Mum wasn't sure she could come. She has been in hospital, you know.'

Well, I did know. Gloria had been in for a chemical peel. Her face still looked a bit raw.

'I didn't want to come unless I could do justice to your big day,' she said grandly. 'And now I can.' She plopped into the chair that Harry had dragged from a nearby empty table. 'Oh, my Lord, you guys, I'm so jet-lagged.' She stretched her thin legs out in front of her. Her high-heeled shoes slipped from her feet.

Now, the thing is, I love my mother. I really do. But I would freak out if she wanted to be friends with my friends. She is my mother, for God's sake. Not my friend. I know some girls call their mothers their best friends. But I think that's odd. Anyway, my ma is older than Gloria O'Hara. She always looks

OK for her age. But she sure isn't some kind of ancient sex symbol.

When I'm sixty-two I want to look good for my age. I want people to think that I could be anything from thirty-five to fifty-five. I'd prefer thirty-five, of course. Not quite sixty. But I certainly don't want to look like a teenage prom queen. Close up, Gloria was just a little bit scary, with her wide-awake eyes and peeled face.

'I didn't realise you were thinking of coming at all,' I said.

'I was at his first wedding,' said Gloria. 'To that silly, silly girl. The least I could do is come to this one. Which I hope will be forever. Which I know will be forever, dearest Jennifer. I know you're the right girl for him.'

Katy and the other girls smiled. But Sarah made a face at me.

Harry waved at the wine waiter. He asked him to bring us a bottle of champagne. Gloria rested her feet on his lap. I wondered why he had invited his mother and never said a word to me about it.

I didn't ask him right away. We stayed up late that night. Despite Gloria's jet-lag, she stayed up late too. She drank lots of champagne – more than me. Then Harry played the piano while she sang Shirley Bassey songs. When she sang 'Diamonds Are Forever' she held up my hand and showed off my engagement ring. I didn't like it one little bit!

It was nearly two in the morning before Harry and I were alone in Room 105. Gloria was safely locked away in 212. I'd been terrified that her room would be next door. But it was further down the hillside. It was out of hearing distance. Which was a good thing. Because I started to shout at Harry.

'Why the hell did you ask your

mother to come and not tell me?' I demanded.

Harry looked at me in astonishment. 'What's the matter with you?' he asked. 'Why are you getting your knickers in a twist?'

'Harry!' I cried. 'She's your mum. We decided against asking our families. It was friends only.'

'Crikey, Jen, keep your hair on.' Harry looked at me in surprise. 'It's different for you. You've got both parents, four sisters and two brothers! You see each other all the time. I'm the only one who sees Mum regularly. I couldn't leave her out.'

'But you didn't tell me!' I wailed. 'I wasn't expecting to see her. It was a surprise.'

'Sure. But a nice surprise.'

I said nothing. Harry and I didn't talk about his mother much. I admired his sense of responsibility towards her.

There are loads of blokes who wouldn't bother to call in to see their mum on the way home from work every evening. But I sometimes felt as though Harry bent over backwards to look after her. After all, she had a life of her own. She went out with 'the girls' a lot. She wasn't always there when he called in. She didn't really need him. I said this to Harry once. He told me that he wanted to be sure Gloria felt looked after. When we got married, he wouldn't have as much time to be with her.

I was relieved to hear that. I had wondered whether Gloria had been part of the problem between Harry and Karen. But I decided I was wrong.

After all, Karen wasn't a very nice person. She was bitchy and unpleasant whenever she phoned Harry. She had probably been horrible to Gloria too. It would be different with me and Harry and Gloria. I could get to like her. And

I would be understanding when Harry went to see her.

So that night I told Harry that I was sorry. I was a bit tired. And maybe jet-lagged. I said that I was pleased that Gloria was going to be at the wedding. Even though I didn't really mean it.

★

'She is a horror,' Dee said to me the night before the wedding. It was barbecue night at the hotel. They had set it up on the beach and it was lovely. We had loaded up our plates with chicken wings, sausages and burgers. Now we were walking back to the tables around the pool. It was better to eat beside the pool. There were sand flies on the beach at night. I didn't want to get bitten by them. Not before my wedding!

'I don't see her that often,' I told Dee. 'I know Harry has to because she's on her own. But I don't see her that much.'

26

'She's a cross between Bet Lynch and a drag queen,' said Dee. Dee was a fan of *Coronation Street* and gossip magazines. 'And a few years from now she'll be even worse.'

I grinned.

'No, seriously,' said Dee as we sat down at the table. 'Where's she going in that get-up?'

I watched my future mother-in-law totter towards the barbecue. She was wearing spiky heels and a leopard-skin dress. It was a tasteful leopard-skin dress … Well, it wasn't a mini or anything like that. It had a long layered skirt and fairly decent chest cover. She had pinned up her blonde hair. She had bought the clip in the hotel shop that morning. It was in the shape of a flamingo and brightly coloured.

'She isn't so bad, really,' I murmured. 'Over the top, but hey, she's colourful.'

'That's true,' said Dee dryly.

Gloria kept us entertained all evening. Her stories were quite funny. But it seemed wrong that she was the star of the show. Maybe I was put out because I thought I should be the star of the show. I was the bride, after all. Then I told myself not to be so bitchy. She was Harry's mother and she was a widow. She was probably lonely. And maybe if I was her age and looked like her, I would want to be the star of the show too. I could see where Harry got his party-loving nature from. Gloria was a real party animal. I was a bit creeped out when the two of them did the tango together. Then Gloria danced with all of Harry's male friends. I danced with Harry. I was glad to have him to myself for a minute.

The music slowed down. He pulled me closer to him and kissed me. When we parted I smiled at him. 'I love you,' I said.

'I love you too,' he told me. He looked over my shoulder. Then he laughed.

'What?' I asked.

'Mum and Dave are looking very smoochy together.'

'What!' I tried to turn around.

He laughed again. 'All in fun, sweetie. All in fun.'

★

I feel bad about saying that I was beginning to hate Gloria. But I couldn't help it. I couldn't seem to get away from her. She was everywhere. On the beach she wore more leopard-print stuff. She also loaded on gold chains, earrings and rings. She bought a toe ring in one of the shops in town. She wore it every day. She laughed and joked with everyone. And she made me feel like I was the old person and she was the younger one. That was because I refused to go on the Pirate Cruise around the island. It was the day before our wedding. I wanted to spend it quietly. I planned to drink lots of water so that my skin would look good. I didn't want to get drunk on free cocktails. (That had happened a few days earlier!) I didn't want to look hungover on my wedding day.

'Maybe you're right,' she said eventually. 'You probably do need some extra work on your looks.'

OK, that was going too far. I know that I'm no Kate Moss. But I'm not that bad. I didn't need to be lectured by someone who couldn't even frown properly!

'Oh, sod off, Gloria,' I said. 'Nobody asked you. And you're one to talk! You probably have a trowel with you for all your make-up.' And I got up and went back to the room. I poured myself a large glass of water and took it out to the balcony. I stretched out on my sun-lounger with a magazine and waited for Harry to join me. He had been there when Gloria had made her remark about my looks. I knew that he would make her say sorry. But I wanted him to comfort me first.

Half an hour later, he still hadn't come. I was beginning to get annoyed. An hour and I was starting to worry. After an hour and a half I stomped back to the beach.

Sarah and Dee were sitting at the water's edge. They hadn't been around when I had spoken sharply to Gloria. Winston was paddling in front of them. He had been there. There was no sign of Harry, Gloria or the others.

'They went on the Pirate Cruise,' Winston told me. 'Gloria really wanted to go and Harry gave in.'

I gritted my teeth and didn't look at Sarah and Dee. They seemed to know

31

what had happened earlier. Winston
must have told them.

'What time are they due back?' I
asked.

'Not till six,' said Winston.

I got up again. 'I'm going to the spa,'
I said. 'I need a relaxing treatment.'

*

It was always busy in the spa. Usually
you had to book days in advance. But I
needed something. I liked the sound of
a wrap. I had read about one which
sounded fantastic in the brochure. It
had mangos and orange blossom and
stuff like that in it. I felt as though I
needed something absolutely fantastic.
It would take my mind off the fact that
Harry and Gloria were on the Pirate
Cruise. I just knew that it would be a
drunken party. I had seen people
coming back from the Pirate Cruise
before. It was free beer all day, for
heaven's sake! Harry wouldn't be able

to say no. And he would be the one looking hungover in the morning.

I was still angry when I arrived at the spa. I asked about the wrap at reception but Marilou shook her head. They were totally booked up for wraps. She said I could have one the day after tomorrow.

The day after tomorrow was no good. I needed to be relaxed and beautiful for my wedding. The day after didn't matter. Well, it did. But I wasn't interested in the day after tomorrow. I was interested in today. I wanted to be wrapped right now! I wanted someone to be nice to me. I wanted to smell of mangos and orange blossom.

'Tanya could give you a massage in half an hour.' Marilou was consulting her book. 'She only has thirty minutes, but that should be enough to relax you.'

So I stayed and had the relaxing massage. Afterwards I did feel a lot better. I wasn't half as angry as I headed back to the room. I sat on the lounger on the patio again and it was nice. I read my book and drank lots of water. I managed to stay fairly relaxed until I saw the catamaran pull up to the beach. It was the return of the Pirate Cruise. I took a deep breath and walked back to the beach.

Gloria was wearing a bandana around her head and a patch over one eye. Maybe she needs it, I thought. Maybe the Botox has worn off. You see, I hadn't really got over it. I was still annoyed with her!

'Hey, there you are!' she cried as she flounced onto the beach. 'You should have come with us. We missed you.'

'I was in the spa,' I told her with dignity. 'I had a treatment booked.'

'I didn't know that,' said Harry as he

arrived beside her. 'I thought you'd been plucked and prepped already.'

I made a face at him.

'Anyone for cocktails?' Gloria waved at a passing waitress. 'How about rum punch for everyone?' She ordered a large jug. I asked the waitress for a bottle of still water. This time I did feel like a party pooper.

Everyone was having a good time. Gloria was telling pirate stories. She was good at telling stories and they were funny. I couldn't help laughing, even though I was still a bit angry. Harry watched her proudly.

'You'd never think it, would you?' he murmured to me while she did her *Pirates of the Caribbean* impressions.

'Think what?' I was thinking lots of things about Gloria.

'You know. That she was a mum. That she'd had a hard life. That Dad died and left her on her own.'

I wanted to say that lots of women had hard lives and were left on their own. But I didn't. In many ways he was right. Gloria was an amazing woman.

★

I had planned to spend a couple of hours with Dee and Sarah that evening. Then Gloria announced that she had booked a table for 'the girls' in the Mariner's Reef. The girls were me and her, Katy and Bella, Sarah and Dee. I was beginning to get seriously pissed off with this woman. She was taking over my whole wedding. But I was afraid to say anything to Harry. He loved the idea of his mum being one of the girls.

We met in the restaurant at eight. The girls seemed to agree with Harry that Gloria was wonderful. (Sarah and Dee didn't, thank goodness. We had already had a bitch about her in the bar. I was still drinking only water. But they were on the cocktails again.) But at dinner everyone discussed Gloria's nips and tucks. That's a totally gross conversation to have when you're eating! Bella and Katy asked her for the name of her favourite surgeon. There was a big debate over the issue of boob jobs. Gloria hadn't had a boob job – yet! But she admitted to lots of Botox. As if we couldn't guess!

'Though really what makes the most difference is the cosmetic stuff,' she told us. 'Look, I had my eyelids tattooed. It means I don't have to worry about eyeliner ever again.'

I shuddered.

'So,' I said eventually. 'You got lots of work done, Gloria. You look so great. Do you think there is any chance that you'll get married yourself one day soon?'

Everyone went quiet. Gloria looked at me. She wasn't laughing any more. 'I really don't think so,' she said icily. 'My

SHEILA O'FLANAGAN

husband and I had a wonderful marriage for over thirty years. I have no need for another man.'

'Use it or lose it,' I told her. I probably shouldn't have said that. But I had given up on the water. I had switched to red wine. Which probably wasn't a good idea.

'Really, Jennifer.' This time her look was one of disgust. 'I don't think that's the sort of thing we want to hear.'

Wasn't it? I had have thought she would be up for a bit of sexy conversation.

'Come on, Gloria,' I said. 'You get tarted up like a dog's dinner every day. Surely it's not all for your own benefit?'

For once Gloria seemed lost for words. Unfortunately I wasn't.

'I mean,' I continued, 'what's with all the leopard-print if not to attract them and pounce?'

Dee gasped. I could see that Katy wanted to laugh.

'You're great for a woman of your

38

age,' I continued. 'But it must be such an effort every day.'

'I beg your pardon.' I could hear the fury in Gloria's voice. 'I'm lucky to have naturally good bone structure. All my procedures have been minor.'

'Minor liposuction?' I snorted. 'I thought lipo meant shoving a tube into you. I thought it sucked out all your fat. I'd hardly call that minor.'

The girls weren't amused now. They were looking at both of us warily. They knew I had gone too far. I knew it too. But I didn't care.

'I have never been so insulted in all my life,' snapped Gloria. 'After all the trouble I went to tonight … I don't know what my Harry sees in you.'

She got up and swept from the room. Her heels were very high. They clicked on the tiled floor. Then she stumbled at the top of the steps. A waiter helped her up again.

'Crikey, Jen,' said Sarah. 'I think you've blotted your copy-book with the ma-in-law.'

I bit my lip. I hadn't originally set out to insult her, but …

'I'll talk to Harry if you like,' offered Bella. 'Tell him you had a bit too much to drink.'

'I haven't had too much to drink,' I lied. 'I'll sort this out myself.'

The men were having their own dinner in the Green Garden. I didn't bother interrupting them. Harry didn't need to know yet. I headed back to the room. Then I stretched out on the big bed. I was asleep almost immediately.

The sound of the door opening woke me up again. I could see the time on the bedside clock. It was nearly midnight. I blinked as the light was switched on. Then I sat up on the bed.

'Hi.' I looked at Harry. I knew my eyes were probably puffy. Red wine makes them go like that. 'It's late.'

'Yes. Well.' He looked at me and I could see he was angry. 'I had to spend some time talking to Mum. She is very upset, you know.'

'Upset? Why?'

'You surely aren't so drunk that you don't remember being extremely rude to her?' he said.

I rubbed my eyes and ran my fingers through my hair. 'I'm sorry about that,' I said. 'It's just … well …' I couldn't think of what to say.

'She is very sensitive,' said Harry.

I thought Gloria O'Hara was as sensitive as a rhino. If she was all that sensitive, she wouldn't have come to the wedding.

'Look, I know you think she is tough and gorgeous,' said Harry. I blinked at

41

him. 'But she isn't at all, really. And it's been hard for her since my dad died.'

'I understand that,' I said. 'It's just ...' I still couldn't think of what to say.

'She only has me, really,' Harry continued. 'Helen doesn't get home very much. Luke isn't good for dropping by either. They have their own lives. She depends on me.'

'I know,' I said. 'And I think it's great the way you do so much for her. I ... well ... I find her a bit overwhelming, that's all.'

'Oh, Jen, you find everything overwhelming!' He laughed. 'You know what you're like. You hate going to parties. You hate dressing up. You hate having to be nice to people ...'

'That's not true!' I cried. 'I don't hate any of those things. I just have to fit them into my life. I thought you understood that.'

'I do, I do,' he said quickly. 'But you've got to realise that Mum is like me. She enjoys life and socialising. But she also feels very strongly about the people she loves.' He looked at me. His dark eyes were gentle. 'So you've got to cut her some slack.'

'I did have a bit too much to drink,' I admitted.

'That's my girl,' he said. 'Now all you have to do is pop down to her room and tell her you're sorry. Then everything will be fine. And you two will be the best of friends again.'

I didn't want to go and apologise to Gloria. But I knew that it was important to Harry. So I put on a pair of shorts and a T-shirt. Then I walked down the little path to Room 212. I knocked on the door. Gloria was wearing a flimsy nightie. It was covered by a silk robe. She was smoking a cigarette. I thought to myself that if she gave up smoking it would be better for her than all the Botox!

I still didn't want to apologise. But I did. She was surprisingly nice to me. She hugged me and called me her new daughter. She told me that we were going to be a great family. Then she asked if I'd like to see her wedding outfit. She said that she had intended it to be a great surprise. But because we were now best friends, she wanted to show it to me. I was terrified at what it might look like. But it wasn't too bad actually. It was mauve silk. It was rather low cut so that her boobs showed. But it was quite stylish. Of course she had a hat too. It was huge. That wasn't a bad thing, I thought. It would hide her face! She had a matching pair of shoes. They had really high heels. Gloria told me that high heels flattered her legs. And her ankles. She said she was proud of her legs and ankles.

'I'm really looking forward to this,' she told me. 'You'll be so much better for Harry than Karen. She was a desperate creature.'

'I hope I will be just right for him,' I said.

'Of course you will,' she told me. 'Karen had no idea about marriage. She gave Harry such a hard time.'

'Did she? How?'

'She nagged him all the time. She got pregnant straight away. She tried to tie him to the house. She hated him being out. She freaked out every time he called to see me.'

I couldn't actually blame Karen for that. I wondered whether or not Gloria would think I was a horrible nag too. It seemed to me that nobody would ever really be good enough for Harry. Not in Gloria's view. I didn't want to stay in the room any longer. I had to escape. I told her that her outfit was gorgeous and that the wedding would be wonderful. When I got back to our room, Harry was already asleep.

★

I had a hangover the next morning. With a pounding headache. My eyes felt gritty too. It seemed that all of the treatments over the past four days had been a complete waste of time and money. I had undone all the good work by drinking red wine. I felt miserable. I blamed myself for being so stupid. I sat at the basin in the hairdressing salon and tried to relax as Tanya massaged shampoo onto my head.

I shifted my neck on the cold ceramic of the basin. My heart was thumping in my chest. Usually it thumped like that when I was nervous. But I wasn't in the slightest bit nervous about the wedding. Maybe it was just the excitement. It was hard to believe that the day was finally here.

On the first day we had arrived, I had booked time in the beauty salon for everyone. But of course I hadn't booked time for Gloria. And I didn't think about it afterwards. It didn't matter. She arrived down about fifteen minutes after the rest of us. She gave Marilou instructions on what had to be done to turn her into a goddess. When we were finished everyone charged their treatements to their room. My bridal make-up was on the house. That was part of the Wedding in Paradise package. I was standing behind Gloria when she signed her name. I noticed that she had filled in Room 105 for the bill. Not her own room number.

'That's our room number,' I pointed out to her.

'Oh, sorry,' she said. 'Still, makes no difference.'

It did make a difference. I didn't want to pay for Gloria's treatments. I said nothing. I felt terrible for suddenly being overcome by meanness. I'm not a mean person. Not normally. I didn't know why I was feeling so mean today. After all, it was my wedding day! I should be feeling completely different. I didn't say anything else to Gloria. Instead, I hurried back to our room. Harry was moving out to give me space to get ready. He was getting ready in Bob's room. Bob was the best man. Harry whistled at my hair-do.

'You look good enough to eat,' he said.

I grinned at him. 'But not now. You'll mess my hair.'

'It's fabulous,' he said. 'You'll be the absolute belle of the ball.'

'Well, after your mother,' I told him.

He laughed. 'Does she look cracking?'

'She looks very Gloria,' I said. 'Oh, by the way, she charged her make-up to our room.'

'Well, that doesn't matter,' said Harry.

'I know, I know,' I said. 'It's just … well … so as you know, I didn't have extra hair-dos or whatever.'

'That's OK,' he said. 'Anyway, we're looking after Mum.'

I frowned. 'Looking after her?'

'Her room,' he explained.

I looked at him in puzzlement. 'How?'

'How do you think, Jen?' He looked at me as though I was a complete idiot. 'The bill, of course.'

I stared at him. 'We're paying the bill for your mum?'

'Of course.'

'But … but …' I was shocked. Last night Gloria had ordered half a dozen bottles of champagne. Champagne wasn't covered by our all-inclusive deal. I had been **to**uched by the gesture because it was very expensive. I had told myself that she was a generous

49

woman at heart. But she wasn't being generous. Harry was. Or *we* were! We were splitting the bill between us, after all. Please believe me when I tell you that it wasn't the cost that bothered me so much. (Though I hadn't budgeted for an extra six bottles of champagne!) It was just that Gloria was spending our money as though it was hers.

'What?' he asked.

'Well, it's just … if we are paying for your mum, why aren't we paying for mine too?' I asked.

He laughed. 'It's a totally different situation,' he said.

'I don't see how.'

'I told you before,' he said patiently. 'My mum is on her own. She depends on me. I want her to feel happy. Besides, you didn't want your mum here. I did want mine.'

What could I say? He was right. I had to learn to compromise.

I shrugged. Harry smiled and kissed me. Harry is a great kisser. Soon we were doing more than kissing. And I wasn't really worrying too much about my hair.

★

But later I started to worry again. I had always thought it was nice how much Harry cared for Gloria. Now I was thinking that it was too much. He thought about her feelings more than mine. She could do no wrong in his eyes. He wanted everything to be perfect for her. I was beginning to think that she mattered more to him than I did. I hadn't ever felt like that before. Sometimes I had been annoyed by her. She had a habit of ringing up out of the blue. Next thing Harry would have to call around to her. Maybe to fit a plug or check a blockage in the plumbing for her. I thought it was crazy that she couldn't fit a plug herself. It's not that hard! But some women are fairly hopeless at that sort of stuff. She was one of them. So I put up with him calling around to her. Even though it was annoying. Even though it was inconvenient.

But this was different. Inviting her and not telling me. Paying for her without telling me either. Doing what *she* wanted all the time. This was just too much! And it wasn't about the money. Money didn't matter when you were talking about your wedding day. After all, I had spent a fortune on my dress!

I looked at my watch. Half-past three. A half hour to go. Sarah and Dee were going to be my bridesmaids. They would be here any minute. I sat on the edge of the bed in my gorgeous dress. I asked myself if I was doing the right thing. If marrying Harry was right for me.

I stood up. The skirt of the dress knocked Harry's mobile phone off the locker. I picked it up. He has a much flashier phone than me. I switched it to camera mode and took a photo of myself. And then I looked in his phonebook. Karen's name was there. Just Karen. No surname. I couldn't stop myself. I dialled the number.

She sounded harassed when she answered.

'What?' she demanded.

I blinked.

'What?' she demanded again. I realised that she thought Harry had phoned her. Still, she didn't have to be so rude.

'Hello,' I said. 'I'm Jennifer Wright.'

'Who?' she said. 'Harry? Is that you?'

'Not Harry.' Was the woman completely stupid? I didn't sound like Harry, did I?

'Jennifer,' I repeated. 'Harry's fiancée.'

'Oh,' she said. I could almost see her frown. 'Why are you ringing me? Is something the matter? With Harry?' There was an anxious tone in her voice. Suddenly I wondered if she still loved him despite everything. But no, I thought. She left him. She wouldn't have done that if she loved him.

I told her nothing was the matter. She asked me again why I was calling.

'Well, you see …' I didn't know what to say.

'Hold on,' she said. I heard the receiver being put down. Then she said, 'Go back to bed.' She wasn't talking to me. She was talking to her little girl. It was five or six hours later at home. Time for her daughter to go to bed. 'I'm telling you,' I heard her say. 'Bed now or Santa won't come.'

I stared out at the blue sky. I couldn't believe that it was cold and dark at home. And probably raining. But I was here, in the sun, ready to marry the man I loved.

'Sorry about that,' she said. 'Gigi is overexcited about Christmas.'

'Gigi?'

'My daughter,' she said. There was a slight pause. 'Harry probably calls her Gloria. I can't possibly. I never wanted to give her that name. But he insisted. It gives me the creeps.'

'Oh?'

'You must have met her,' said Karen. 'Gloria. The bitch from hell.'

'Oh, come on,' I said feebly. 'She's not that bad.'

'Hah!' cried Karen. 'You don't think so? Well, maybe she has changed. And if so, good luck to you. But when we were married she ruled our lives. Harry called over to her four nights a week. She wanted him to take her to the movies. Or to her bridge class. He was at her beck and call every single day. She bought stuff I couldn't afford. Why? Because Harry was paying her bills. Out of our joint account. She used to compare herself to me. She would tell Harry that we looked like sisters. Sisters! If that woman was my sister, I'd murder her. And I mean it. I hated the bitch and she hated me too. I hope it's different for you. I really do. But she is going to try to ruin your life. Because no woman is good enough for Harry. Or good enough for her.' Karen finally ran out of breath. And then she said brightly, 'But, sorry, why did you call?'

'Um … well …'

'It's Gloria, isn't it?' said Karen. 'She's there.'

'How did you know?'

'How wouldn't I know?' demanded Karen. 'I remember her at our wedding. Practically pushing me out of the photos. Shoving her boobs at the camera. You know she says she never had them done. I'm not so sure about that. She is far too proud of them.'

'She has had work done over the last few years,' I said. 'But not them as far as I know.'

'It would take more than work to turn her into a decent human being,' snorted Karen.

I giggled. I couldn't help it.

'So, look – is it Gloria?'

I gave in. I told her everything. I told her I felt terrible for thinking that my future mother-in-law was a freeloading cow. For being annoyed that she thought the sun shone out of Harry's ass. And out of her own ass too! I felt bad about thinking that she looked just like Barbie's granny.

Karen laughed. 'That woman made my life hell,' she said. 'I was never good enough for him. And it's a shame. Harry is a decent bloke. But I couldn't always play second fiddle to his mother. I thought it would be different after Gigi was born. It wasn't. Gloria didn't like having a grandchild. She thought it was ageing.'

'Oh.'

'Are you having second thoughts?'

'I'm getting married in less than half an hour,' I told her. 'I can't have second thoughts.'

'Of course you can,' she said. 'Think about living close to Gloria for the rest of your life.'

I shuddered.

'Good luck,' she said.

'Yeah, thanks.' I sat on the bed again. Then Dee and Sarah knocked at the door.

They looked great in their new dresses. They had bought them in Harvey Nicks. Their make-up and hair-dos looked great too. They had brought a bottle of champagne with them. It was the free house champagne. Not the expensive champagne Gloria had ordered.

'You look fantastic!' cried Dee as she popped the cork. 'We've just seen all the lads. Harry looked particularly great.'

I smiled half-heartedly.

'Well,' said Sarah as she raised a glass. 'To the future Mrs O'Hara. May God bless her and all who sail in her.'

My smile was even more half-hearted.

'Hey, Jen, what's up?' She realised I wasn't quite getting into the spirit of things.

I shrugged. 'I … I'm not sure …'

They looked at me shocked.

'Not sure?' repeated Dee.

'I'm just—'

'Having last-minute nerves,' finished Sarah. 'Come on, Jen, love. You know you're crazy about him. You know he is crazy about you. And you're in paradise, for heaven's sake.'

'I know. I know,' I wailed. 'But …' And then I poured out all my reservations about Gloria. I said I was worried about the future. I told them that I had phoned Karen and what she had said.

'But come on, sweetie, she's his ex-wife,' Sarah reminded me. 'Ex-wives never have a good word to say about their husbands.'

'Sometimes they do,' I told her.

They exchanged looks.

'She sounded really nice and normal,' I said, talking about Karen. 'But he always told me she was horrible.'

'You've heard her being horrible,' Dee reminded me. 'What about the message on his phone?'

That was true. I felt a little bit better.

'And Gloria is probably just a bit nervous in front of you too,' added Dee, somewhat less helpfully.

'Yeah, right,' I snapped. 'The woman is a self-centred lunatic.'

This time the looks they exchanged were more than stricken.

'She's a bit … loud, perhaps,' said Sarah finally.

'Would you like her as a mother-in-law?' I demanded.

There was total silence.

'Oh shit,' I said and started to cry.

They begged me to stop or I would wreck my make-up. Then they reminded me once more how great Harry was to me. They reminded me that usually I didn't meet Gloria very often. They said I wouldn't see her very much after this. They told me that I was getting into a state over nothing. Everyone had nightmare mothers-in-law, Sarah said. Everyone.

'Am I being a total fool?' I asked them and they both nodded.

I nodded too. 'I'm sorry,' I said. I rubbed my eyes. The so-called waterproof mascara smudged my face.

'Shit,' said Sarah.

'Oh, God,' I wailed. 'I can't get married like this.'

'Don't worry,' Dee told me. 'It only needs a little repair work.'

'But I'm going to be horribly late,' I wailed.

'I'll leg it down and tell them there was a bit of a make-up hitch,' said Sarah. 'By the time I'm back again you'll be ready.'

'OK,' I said as she whirled out of the room.

I felt calm again. The crisis had passed. Yes, Gloria was overwhelming. But no, she wouldn't overwhelm my life. Harry loved me. I loved Harry. That was all that mattered.

The mobile phone rang. Dee was so

startled that she stabbed me in the eye with the mascara.

I rubbed my eye. Then I picked up the phone.

'Are you still there, Jennifer?' It was Karen.

'Yes.'

'Look,' she said. 'I feel bad about the things I said. You go and marry Harry. Have a great life with him. Don't worry about Gloria. You can deal with her.'

'Why couldn't you?' I asked.

'I was crazy about Harry,' she told me. 'He is a great guy. And I loved him. But he was weak when it came to Gloria and I couldn't take it. He never said no to her and …' Suddenly she started ranting about her all over again.

Dee whispered to me to get off the phone. I waved her away. I was listening to Karen. She didn't sound half as horrible as everyone thought. I felt that being married to Harry had been bad for her. Maybe it would be bad for me too.

'Everything's fine.' Sarah came back into the room. 'Harry laughed. Said he knew you'd keep him waiting ...' Then she saw I was on the phone. She made a face at Dee. Dee shrugged her shoulders. The two of them sat on the end of the bed and waited while I listened to Karen.

'Jeez, I'm sorry,' Karen said eventually. 'I guess it still gets to me. And I meant to say to you that everything would be fine.'

'I know,' I said.

'When are you due to marry him?' she asked.

'Fifteen minutes ago.'

'What!' she yelled. 'I'm stopping you marrying him.'

'Of course not,' I said. 'I was going to be late anyway.'

'Thank God.' I could hear the relief in her voice. 'I couldn't bear it if I messed up your life too.'

'Is your life messed up?' I asked.

She sighed. 'Only because I thought it would all be different,' she replied. 'And I couldn't cope with how things turned out. But you sound like a tougher cookie than me. And I bet it will all work out great for you. I do hope so. Really.'

'What about money?' I asked.

'What do you mean?'

'Well, if me and Harry have a kid, maybe he won't have so much for Gigi … for treats and stuff.'

She snorted again. 'He doesn't spend money on Gigi. He only spends it on Gloria.'

'That's not fair! He loves Gigi. I know he buys her stuff. And you get loads …'

'No, I don't,' she said fiercely. 'He

only gives me the bare minimum. It's Gloria he spends it on. He loves Gloria more than Gigi. He loves her more than he ever loved me. The woman can do no wrong in his eyes. A baby cries and poops and gets in the way.'

I thought she was losing it a bit now. But even so …

'Go on,' she said again. 'Everyone knows I'm a bit loopy. You're not. Marry him and be happy.'

'Yes,' I said. 'I will.'

I snapped the phone shut again.

'What was all that about?' demanded Dee.

'Karen again,' I told her.

'Is she trying to nab him back?' asked Sarah. 'Is that it?'

'I really don't think so,' I said. 'She says she loves him but she hates Gloria more.'

Nobody said anything. We were all

wondering whether I hated Gloria more than I loved Harry.

'Will I fix your make-up?' asked Dee.

'Of course.'

I sat on the chair beside the dressing table. She started with the mascara again. Meanwhile, I was thinking. I was marrying Harry, not his mother. I had to remember that.

When Dee had finished my make-up I walked onto the balcony. I could see the guests in the distance. The men would be hot. It wasn't the weather for tuxedos! Gloria would be OK. Her dress was light enough for the heat.

She was standing beside Harry. Then she hugged him.

Harry. Gloria. Gloria. Harry.

Oh, hell, I thought. This wasn't what it was supposed to be like. This was supposed to be the happiest day of my life.

'You ready?' asked Sarah.

I walked back into the room. The two of them were looking at me.

'No.' I tugged at the zip of my dress.

'Jennifer!'

I continued pulling at the zip. When it was down all the way, I stepped out of my dress.

'Jen!' Sarah tried to stop me. 'What are you doing?'

'I've changed my mind,' I told her simply. 'I can't marry Harry and his mother. Would you mind awfully going down and telling them? I think Gloria would probably just kill me. Thanks very much.'

Then I went into the bathroom. I scrubbed my face until none of the make-up remained. Then I poured myself a glass of champagne. I knew I had done the right thing.